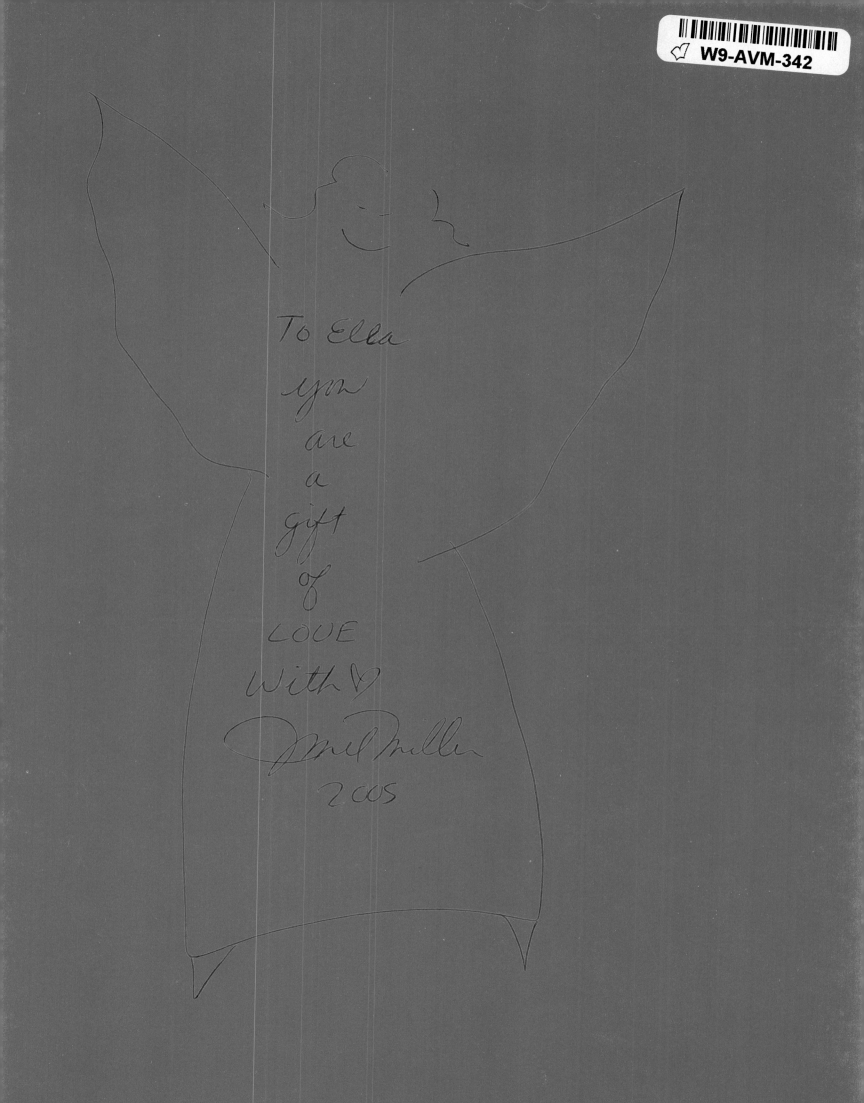

To Ella
you
are
a
gift
of
LOVE
With ♥

[signature]
2005

W9-AVM-342

Angels in the Vineyards
Poetry & Paintings by
Jessel Miller

DEDICATION

I dedicate this book to all the Parents and Grandparents who have opened their hearts to me in my Napa Valley gallery. For twenty years I have listened to their poignant stories and wishes for a calmer, more gentle world and a life which honors the child within us all. I celebrate children and the animals for they are wellsprings of love, and if this book brings a smile to a child's face, I have succeeded in my mission.

I dedicate this book to my best friend and editor, Carolynne Gamble who never fails to help me find my way and my words, and to my husband, Gary for his unwavering belief in my heART.

I thank my pet models, Gobby and Jack, the dogs and Tilly and Tucker, the turtles, and their owners, Carol, Cindi and Hilda who have watched and delighted in the creation of this book. I thank Timmins, Ontario, Canada, the peaceful community where I was born and raised.

Published by Jessel Gallery
Napa, California

By Hand is By Heart

Angels in the Vineyards
Text and Illustration copyrights © 2001 Jessel Miller

No part of this publication may be reproduced, stored in, or introduced
into a retrieval system, or translated, in any form or by any means
(electronic, mechanical, photocopying, recording, or otherwise)
without the prior written permission of Jessel Miller.

ISBN 0-9660381-6-9
Library of Congress Number: 2001092424

10 9 8 7 6 5 4 3 2
Editing by Carolynne Gamble
Typography and electronic prepress by Waterford Graphic Design
Printed by Tien Wah Press, Singapore

Angels in the Vineyard may be ordered directly from:

Jessel Gallery
1019 Atlas Peak Road
Napa, California 94558
888-702-6323 voice
707-257-2350 voice
707-257-2396 fax

jessel@napanet.net
www.jesselgallery.com

Publisher's Cataloging-in-Publication
(Provided by Quality Books, Inc.)

Miller, Jessel

Angels in the vineyards/illustrator, Jessel Miller;
author, Jessel Miller; editor, Carolynne Gamble, --
1st ed.
     p. cm.
     SUMMARY: Angels Ease and Grace take the children back
to their grandparents' time when life was lived at a slower
pace, and the journey was as joyful as the destination.
     Audience: Ages 2-12.
     ISBN 0-9660381-6-9

1. Love--Juvenile fiction. 2. Values--Juvenile fiction.
3. Imagination--Juvenile fiction. 4. Angels--Juvenile fiction.
5. Love--Fiction. 6. Values--Fiction. 7. Imagination--Fiction.
8. Angels--Fiction. 9. Stories in rhyme. I. Title.

PZ8.3.M6156Ang 2001   [E]
                        QB121-154

Angels from the starry sky

Came to earth one day

To take the children back in time

To learn their Grandfolks' way.

They all flew past the lazy moon

Floating in the light

Letting go of all their fears

Feeling sheer delight.

Arriving at a front door

They did not know this place

It's where your Grandma grew up

Said Angels, Ease and Grace.

She lived inside a tiny home

That smelled of fresh baked pies

Grandma quilted by the fire

Love gleaming in her eyes.

Next stop was Grandpa's workshop

Along this journey sweet

All his precious things around

Kept so clean and neat.

Grandpa worked so hard each day

Yet when he came to rest

The animals all gathered 'round

And nestled on his chest.

Many things were done back then

That slowed life down each day

Like taking walks on country roads

The good old-fashioned way.

Plum tree orchards bloomed

And flowers lined the lane

A quiet special feeling

Like listening to the rain.

Ease and Grace in flowers appeared

At each and every turn

Reminding them to take deep breaths

To listen, watch and learn.

The children hugged the Angels

And slipped back to their home

They snuggled safely in their beds

And found this little poem . . .

"Each day a blessed light will shine

To lead you on your way

It's what you do with all your time

That makes a special day.

Don't rush, they whispered softly

Take time to know your place

Be gentle to your Spirit

Respect your time and space.

Be content with what you have

Appreciate your health

Be grateful, fit and happy

This is your greatest wealth."

The children woke next morning

And knew the Angels' wish

No television, no computers

Today they simply . . . fish.

Catch and release...
Catch and release...
A fish mantra...